PiG-MiNT

Story by:

Maurice Bennett

Illustrated by:

Maurice Bennett

ISBN: 978-0-6152-0808-4

Bright and early on Monday morning, a mailman is out on delivery. His very first package is to be delivered to "Big Jake's Slaughterhouse." For the past mile there has been nothing, but dew covered hills and pastures, as far as the eye can see. Then he noticed an old paved road. The road was covered in cracks and the tar was light gray from years of travel. Yet, the road was dormant; grass was growing through the cracks. Given his travel time he figured this was the place. So he made the turn and headed down the road.

Soon a building appeared. The parking lot had two cars in the front. There was an old fenced in holding area. The fence was old and worn like it had been used for a decade and the scent in the air gave signs of the recent animals that were kept within the area. He backed up to the loading dock. The mailman jumped out of the truck and quickly ran up the steps to open the back of the truck. The door slid up quickly. There was a wooden box in front of him with "Big Jake's Slaughterhouse" stamped on the top left of the box. Right next to the stamp was the address. The delivery guy looked around the loading dock and didn't see a sign or a doorbell for the dock. The fenced in area and the smell convinced him it was the right place. He put the box next to him in front of the door and knocked. BOOM, BOOM, BOOM, BOOM, "Delivery!" he shouted. The knocks sounded like thunder on the big metal door. He waited. Then BOOM, BOOM, BOOM, BOOM. The door creaked as he knocked. He could hear the knocks echo into the huge space inside. No one opened the door. He checked his watch and looked up at the sun. He mumbled to himself, "I have to stay on schedule. The box should be okay out here." He closed the back of the truck and locked it quickly. He lowered himself off the edge of the dock and hopped back into the driver seat. The truck rumbled as he started it up. The tires spun as they moved the lumbering vehicle off to its next delivery.

A few moments after the truck drove away the box began to shake as the contents shuffled about. Whatever was in the box was alive. Low grumbles came from inside the box. As they grew louder the grumbles became a frightened squeal. Then CLICK! A loud sound came from the door. It was the sound of the door being unlocked. As the door slowly opened, the box grew silent. The door creaked up as if it were closed for ages. The rusted wheels squeaked and squealed in the agonizing strain of motion. Finally the sound stopped. Footsteps came toward the box. A shadow appeared over outlining a tall slender man wearing a hat. He was wearing a white apron over white pants and a white button down collar shirt. There was a patch on his shirt in red and white stitching. The patch read, "Great Treat Mints…..The peppermint of mints." The same patch was on the hat. There was a cord coming from his pocket going to his ears. He had earphones on. The volume was turned all the way up as the music escaped into the morning air. The man lifted the box onto his shoulder and took it inside. He sat the box down for a moment, so that he could close the door. The door rushed down, closing with a thud at the end. The chain, that is used to open the door, swung back and forth. The taps from the chain hitting the door, slowly faded away as the slender man carried the box down the hall.

The sound of footsteps echoed in the hall as the man made his way to the end. A low hum began to grow louder as he walked farther down the hall. The hall opened to a huge area where it was so loud that all you could hear are the whirring, ticks, clanks, and hissing of machinery. There was a sign hanging high above the middle of the room that read like the patch on the man's shirt. "Great Treat Mints....The peppermint of mints candy factory." This was a candy factory. Not just any candy factory, but a peppermint candy factory. The best peppermint candy in the state was made there. They have just expanded to the area and were up and running. Even though the outside still looked like the slaughterhouse it was before the new owner moved in. The previous owner of the nasty, dirty slaughterhouse factory, "Big Jake's Slaughterhouse," moved two miles down the road to a bigger location. This place was now a candy factory. The man, who was a worker at the factory, walked right through the middle of the open floor with the box.

Maurice Bennett ©2007

He stopped directly in front of a hatch. The hatch was attached to a big machine that kind of looked like a big metal bowl. It had an open top with two metal bars that were reaching into the bowl, circling slowly. A sign next to the hatch read, "MIXER." He sat the box on the floor while he stepped on a stool and opened the hatch. A light mist sprayed out as the man reared back to avoid contact. If the spray had gotten on him, it would never come off. He would be sticky for weeks. He grabbed the box and opened it up quickly, completely removing the front of the box. Then he dumped whatever was in the box into the machine. Normally this box would contain sugar or food coloring for making the candy. But, this time the box does not contain either. Instead, it contained A PIG. The worker just dumped a live, smelly, farm raised, snort-snort, oink-oink pig into the nice, sweet tasting candy mix!

Splash! The candy substance sprang up, as the startled pig hit the bottom of the bowl. He hit the bottom kicking and squealing, as he adjusted to the new surroundings. Then he slowly calmed down and got quiet. The pig took a few moments to get oriented, but it was hard because not a second later one of the metal arms started moving his direction. Slow and efficient, the arms moved quietly around the bottom. Churning the candy until it was just right. At first, the pig tried to move away, but the thick candy mix would not let him move in time. The arm hit the pig and started pushing him around the bowl. Round and round the bowl the pig went. Scared and alone in a strange place the pig tried to find a way out. He tried to climb up the side of the bowl, but it was too slick. Everything was covered in candy mix. He began to realize, that the only way out was to wait until someone came and found him in the candy mix. But, what will happen if someone does see him? What will they do? The pig wondered. Soon, the pig was being moved around the bottom as if he were part of the candy.

Suddenly the arms stopped. The arms slowly retracted out of the bowl. The pig thought that maybe someone had spotted him. So he tried to squeal for help, but the candy has covered him in a thick, sticky coating. It was making it hard for him to shape his mouth to squeal. He strained and strained to get just a squeak out when CHOOM! Something else was happening. The pig froze. The center of the candy mix started to get lower and lower. He slowly began sliding to the center. He was SINKING! The pig turned to try and move to the side of the bowl, but it was no use. The candy was too thick. It would not let him move. He struggled anyway. Before he knew it, he was being sucked down below the candy mix. Soon it was dark and he could not breathe. He tried and tried to struggle, but the machine was too powerful.

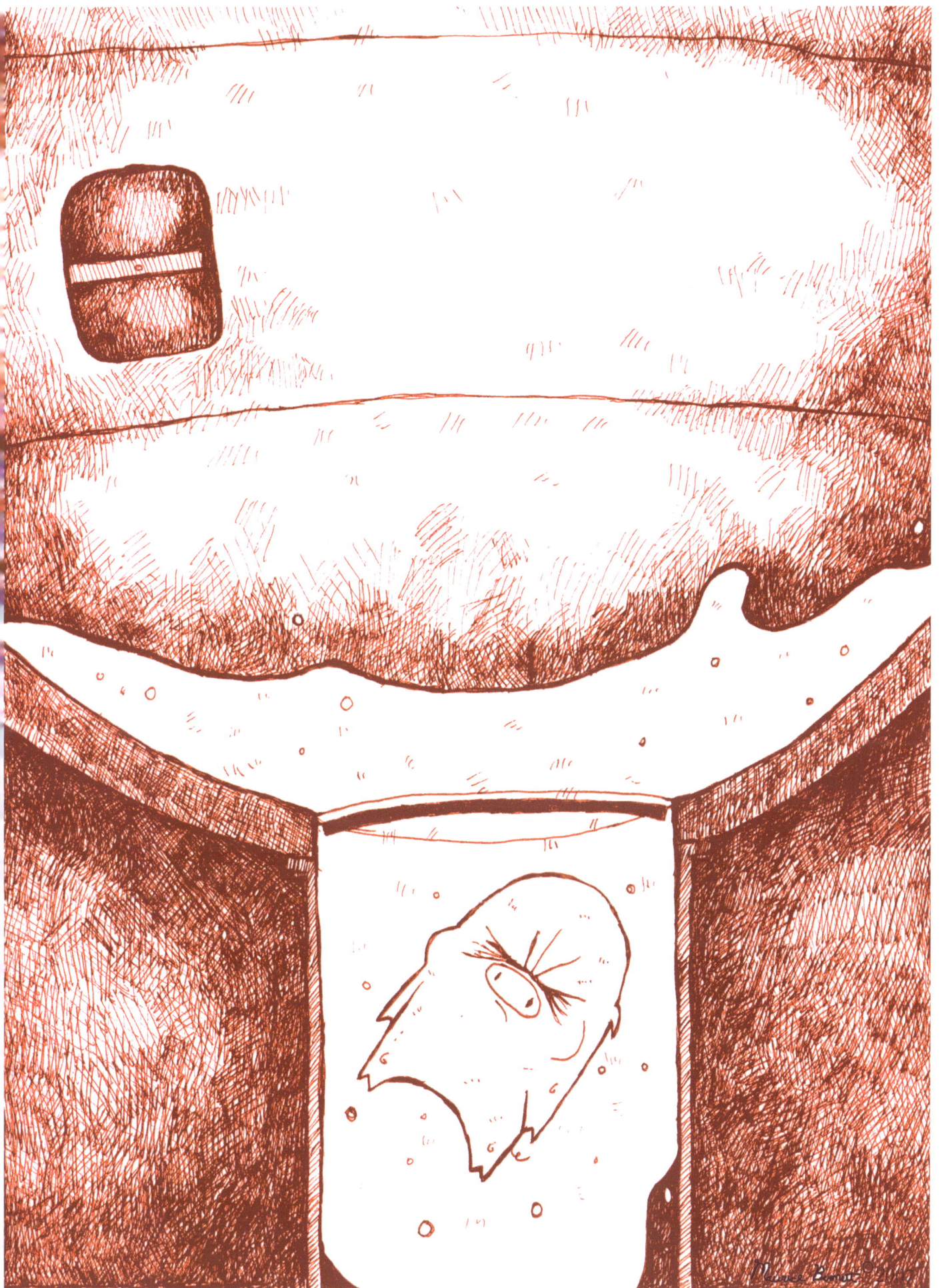

Then....PLOP!.....GASP! The pig took a deep breath of air. As he catches his breath, he took in his surroundings. He realized that he was trapped in a block of thick, doughy, candy mix. He noticed a number of nozzles hanging from the ceiling. The polished chrome tips reflected the pig filled lump of candy mix. He tried to figure out what they were for. Are these the tools that will slaughter me? The pig wondered. He has heard many stories from the farm, about pigs not returning from slaughter. The ones that did return, talked about the horrible things they had seen. Horrible, horrible things. Then SWITCH! The nozzles moved slightly. Have the nozzles seen me in the block of candy? Are they coming to....to.....slaughter me? The pig thought. They slowly moved into position, just over the hardening block of candy. SPLATTER!....Spt!,Spt!........Shhhhhh! The nozzles began to spray fluid all over the block. Then the nozzles sprayed a red colored gooey substance on the candy. They streaked the color back and forth over the block. Then two little doors on the ceiling opened, as the nozzles retreated to their original positions.

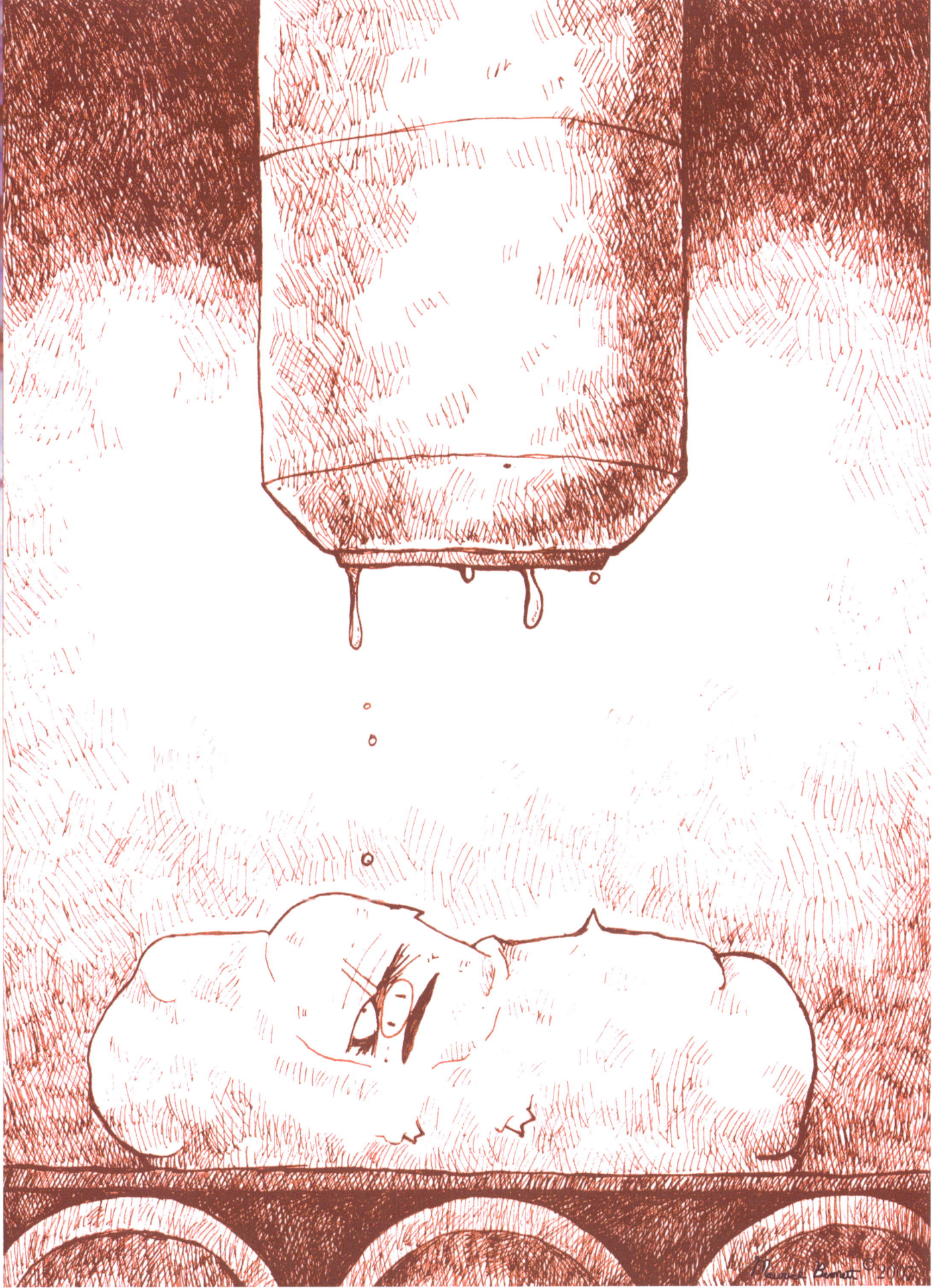

Zzzz, zzzz, zzzzzz. Two mechanical arms extended down from high above to reach each end of the, now striped, candy block. Chink! The crude metal hands opened at the end of the arms to grab each end of the pig filled hunk of candy. The arms began to pull. The pig could feel his body being stretched with the candy. Farther and farther, the arms stretched the candy. The pig tried to let out a squeal, to announce the agony he was feeling, but the candy coating, which became hard as a rock and almost like a glossy finish, would not permit. Farther and farther the arms pulled. Then they came back together causing the candy to fold over. Then one arm let go of the top and grabbed the bottom of the, now folded in half, block of candy. The arms stretched the candy out again. The pig thought, this time they would surely break him. But the arms stopped, after a short stretch. Then one arm rotated one way and the other arm rotated the opposite, twisting the candy block.

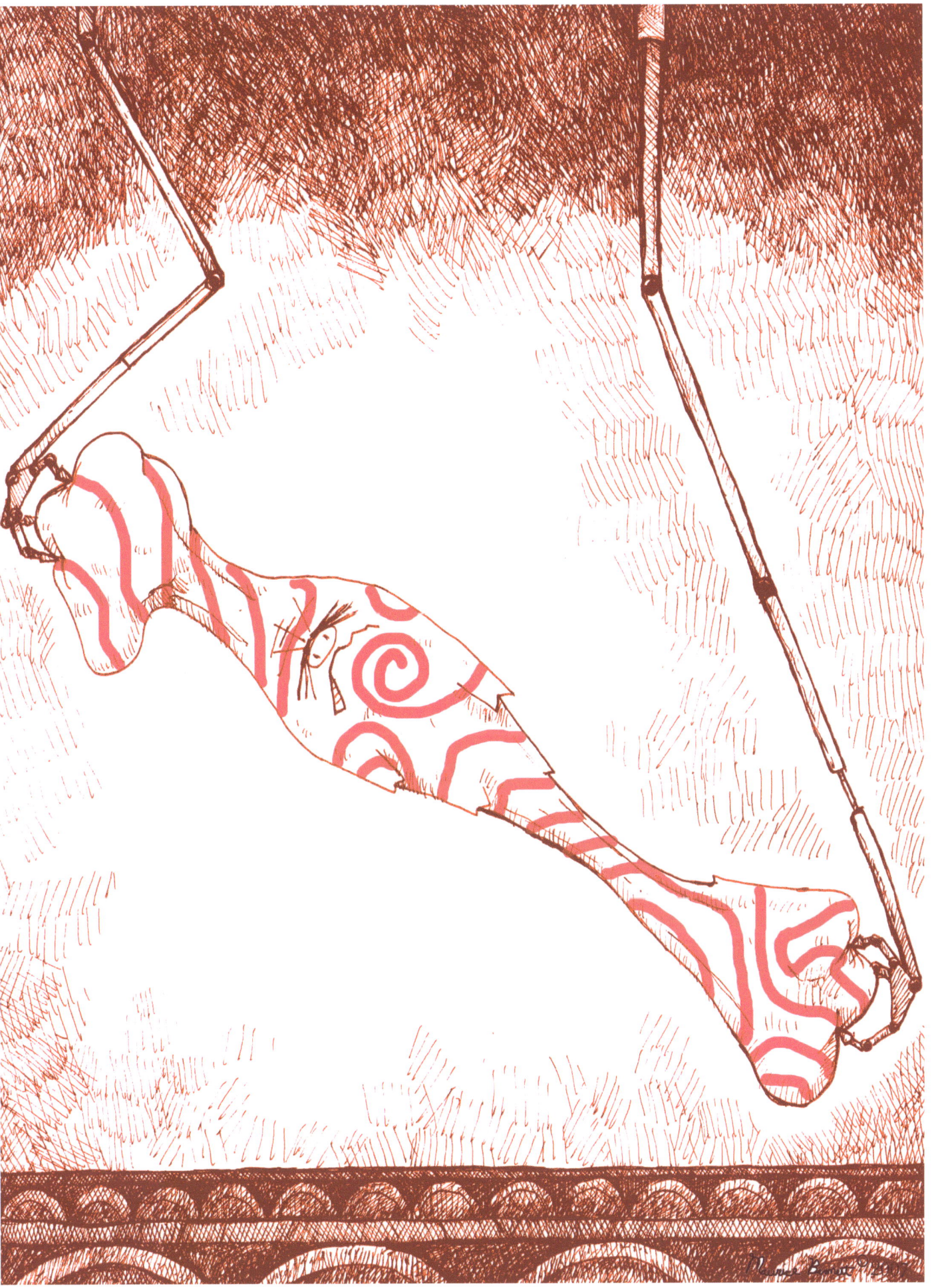

The arms slowly moved the candy twist over to a new table. The new table was black and was moving. The arms lowered the twist onto the moving table. What kind of place is this? The pig wondered. The moving table squeaked, as it moved the twist along. The pig could see the lights above him, come and go and become larger, then smaller as he traveled down the table going from one room to the next. The pig tried to move. But he could only move slightly, since the candy he was wrapped in was starting to become more and more solid. He shifted a little and the twist rocked some. He shifted the other way and the twist rocked some more. He moved just a little more and he managed to shift his weight enough to roll the twist over slightly to the side. This gave him a view of the moving table. So when he looked up, he could see down the table. Quickly his relief, from being able to turn the twist to the side, vanished. The pig wished he had stayed still, so he would not see what was coming towards him.

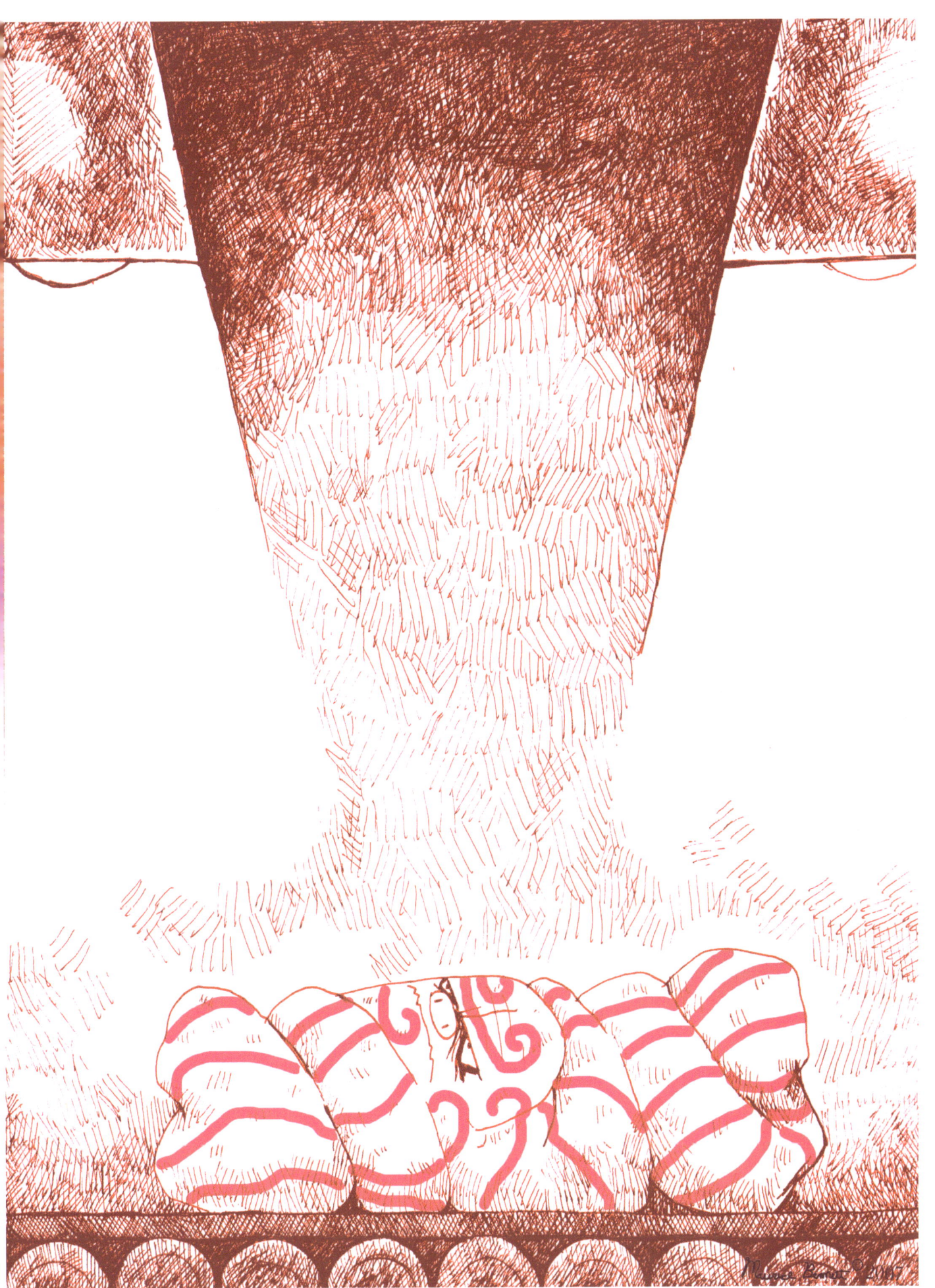

All moving tables have to lead somewhere. This moving table was leading him to a giant metal roller with holes all over it. It was black and it was rolling at the same speed as the table. The roller covered the whole table. Clearly denying any attempt at escaping the inevitable. The pig's eyes stayed locked on the man made object. His eyes widened, as he slowly approached the cold immovable roller. Each light that passed over him, counted down the moments before he met the cruel object face to face. The roller slowed, as it began to press down on the front of the twist flattening out the thick candy. The roller made its way to the pig in the middle. The pig closed his eyes, as the ponderous shadow overtook him. The moving table dipped down, as it moved closer and closer. All of a sudden, he heard a groan as if there was someone in pain. A horrible sound came from the roller. It was the sound of the roller being forced upward. The combination of the pig and thick candy caused the roller to stress and strain as it lifted up and over the pig in the middle. The roller slammed down as it pressed the rest of the candy twist into tiny, little, circular mints.

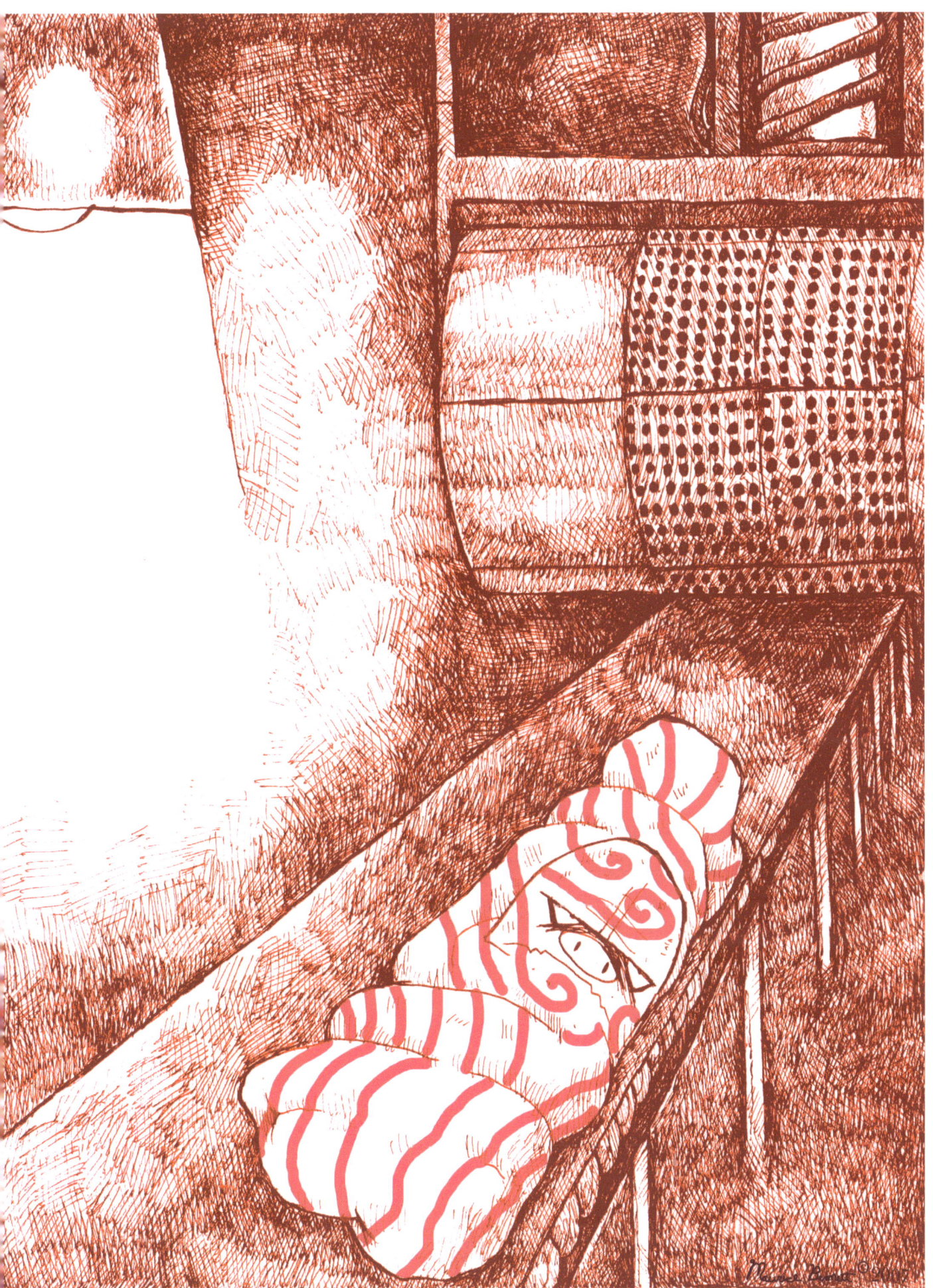

The pig found himself surrounded by little candies on the moving table. The roller freed the pig of the candy twist that was around him. He could not move his front legs or open his mouth, but his back legs were free. The hard candy coating kept him stiff, as the moving table pressed on. Besides being in the candy coating, the ride on the moving table was not half bad. He started enjoying it. At least he was still alive. Then CHOM! A door opened up ahead. The pig couldn't see where the door was at first but he did notice that the moving table was ENDING! The pig tries to scoot and hop, to keep from going over the edge of the table, but it was no use. The candy coating was too stiff. All he could manage was a tiny hop in the opposite direction from the edge of the table. The edge was coming fast. So he tried again. One hop..........
Two hop........Three hoooooooooooop!

The pig was dropped down a metal chute. He could hear a strange clanging then.....CLANG! He hit a metal slide. Down, down the pig slid, as he fell into a place unknown. Suddenly he came to a stop inside a strange rotating machine. The machine hummed quietly as it moved ever so slowly. The gentle motion began to roll the pig around. Round and round and round. Over and over and over. The remaining candy pieces that followed the pig on his detour could be heard sliding around on the metal surface. The misty spray hissed as it came from little holes in the machine that was making the candy coating shiny and less sticky. Then the machine shifted. He could see the light travel across the tiny space, as the opening was being redirected. Suddenly he was sliding towards the opening. Normally, the pig would try to escape. But this time, he knew his efforts would not work since the candy was now as hard as a rock. So the pig closed his eyes and just glid.

Thud! The pig landed on another moving table. He opened his eyes and breathed a sigh of relief. A little glimmer of hope began to fill his heart. He thought that he may make it out of this mess. But then....AAAAANNNN! The pig was shaken from the horrific sound. He looked ahead. Oh no! Just when things started to look up he sees the most enormous, gigantic, menacing, terrifying, machine he has seen yet. The machine shot steam from its back. Its belly grumbled and rattled from its moving parts. It's flashing red eyes pierced through the steam like lasers. It sends a shiver down the back of the little pig. He is frozen in fear. It's a monster! The moving table slowly moves towards the great machine. As he gets closer he could here the horrific sounds of what was happening inside of its belly. A strange crackling sound echoed from within the machine. Soon the pig was right in front of the great mechanical monstrosity. Its teeth flapped back and forth like limp noodles. Its breath smelled of a foul stench. The smell......

Burned the pig's nostrils. The pig's heart pounded. His breath was short. His chest ached from the internal stampede as he was transferred into the mouth of the beast.

It was dark at first. Then everything turned completely red. A dark shadow grabbed the pig and lifted him off the table. The shadow dropped him onto an invisible blanket. Soon the pig was trapped. The blanket was around him so tightly, he could see his breath on the blanket clouding his vision. The temperature began to rise. The pig could feel the blanket getting smaller. It cracked and crumpled as its grip tightened. The belly of the beast was like an oven. The pig could feel his hold on reality slipping. Everything became a blur, as the pig drifted into a dream. AAAAAANNNNNN! The pig's eyes popped open. He was disoriented at first, but soon started to remember. THE BEAST! His eyes searched desperately for the monster. It was gone. He started to think that it was all a dream, but he felt the moving table beneath him. The invisible blanket was still wrapped around him. Its grip had loosened slightly, so the pig could breathe a little easier. So the beast must have either spit him out and left, or........or......dropped him from the other end. Disgust overwhelmed the pig, as he began to understand the crudeness of waste. He had never felt so low.

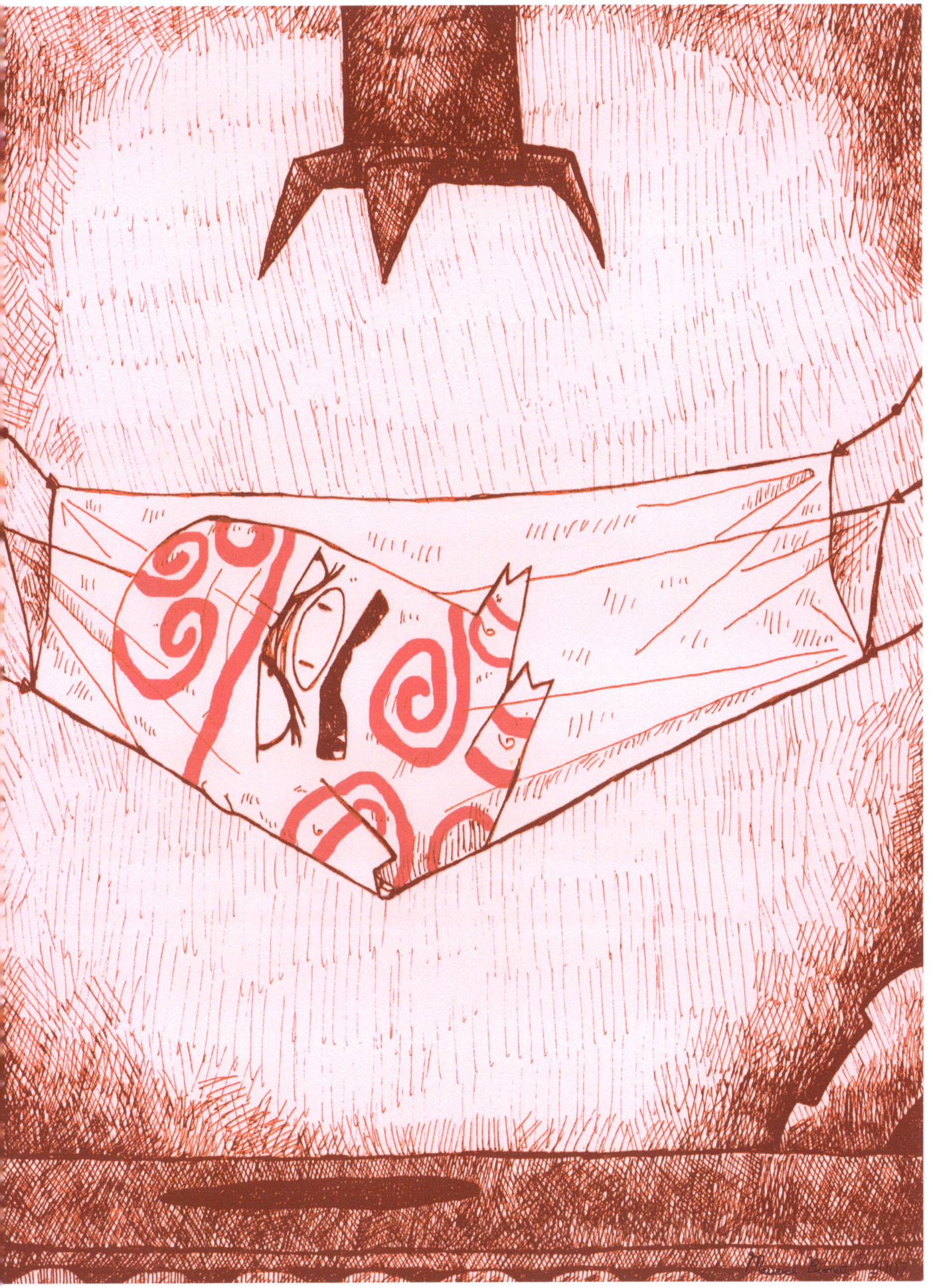

The moving table carried the pig to another room full of boxes stacked to the ceiling. An open box sat at the end of the table, half full of little mint candies. The pig went over the edge of the table, into the box. The candy cushioned the fall of the plastic wrapped, candy coated pig. Slowly, the box filled up with mints. Chom. The moving table stopped. All the machines stopped moving. It was completely quiet in the entire factory. Footsteps began to echo in the room. Music faded into the room as the footsteps came closer to the box. It was the factory worker again and he was carrying a roll of packaging tape. He looked down at his walkman to make sure the volume was all the way up. Kkkkkrrrrrrkkk! He pulled a piece of tape off the roll and placed one end on the top of the box. Then he closed the flaps and puts the tape down over them. The pig could hear the commotion going on outside the box. The worker used the tape a few more times then the commotion stopped. All of a sudden, the mints started to shift around. The worker picked the box up and carried it out of the room. This time, the worker carried it in front of him to support the weight of it.

The mints rattled back and forth, as the worker walked to the back of the room. At the back of the room was a wooden stand about eight inches tall from the floor. The stand had two holes in the front of it and a bunch of boxes stacked on top of it. The worker used his knee to lift the box up shoulder height and placed the box on the end of the top row, completing the stack of boxes. Silence started to settle inside the box, as the little candy coated pig lay in seclusion amongst the tiny mints. As the last few mints finished settling, another sound began to fade in.

Beep........beep.......Beep.........BEEP!..........Bump, Bump. The box began to slightly rock side to side and bumped to a halt. Then the rocking continued. A forklift was moving the stack of boxes to the loading dock. The huge door, that greeted the little pig at the delivery that morning, is now open wide. The door let the outside sunlight into the room.

The forklift slowly went out on to the loading dock, with the stack of boxes raised up high. The wheels stopped squeaking, as they left the tile floor. A white truck was parked in front of the dock with the engine still running. The air smelled of exhaust, as the truck idled with its back door open, eagerly anticipating the stack of boxes. The forklift rose as it drove across the ramp connecting the dock platform to the delivery truck. The boxes shifted, as the forklift came to a stop in the back of the truck. The air smelled like dust and mold. The truck was stuffy and had other box stacks with white pieces of paper taped on the front of the stacks. The forklift was about five feet from one of the stacks. The lift gently lowered the stack, from the factory, on to the floor of the truck. The beeping noise started again, as the vehicle backed slowly out of the truck. The back of the truck creaked as it recovered from the weight of the fork lift. The factory worker drove the lift back into the factory. After a few minutes, the door to the back dock came thundering down to a hard stop as it hit the floor. The feint sound of the chain, used to open the door, tapped as it swung back and forth.

The delivery truck idled quietly. Occasionally, the engine's pace would quicken as it tried to keep the temperature in the cab cool.

The driver sat in the air conditioned cab listening to a tape, to increase his self esteem. He was balding and his button down shirt was a little sweaty and slightly un-tucked. The shirt read, "We deliver." His slacks were clean except for a little dust spot on the front of his pants. He was breathing slowly and heavily to the commands of the tape. His eyes were closed and his index finger and thumb were pressed together. His hands were raised just above his waist. He took a deep, deep breath and held it for a few moments. Then, as he exhaled he opened his eyes. He told himself, speaking in the lowest of tones, that he could do it. He could weather any storm life threw at him. He reached down to put the truck into gear, when he noticed a light on the dashboard. He paused for a second to figure out what it was. Then he said, "Oh Jeez! I gotta do everything!" He unlocked the door lock and kicked the door open. The driver hopped out irritated and mumbled to himself as he stormed to the back of the truck to close the door. He climbed the steps to the dock and walked up to the back of the truck. He stopped and looked up at the strap hanging from the door. With a scowl on his face he dipped down to muster the energy for a one time jump for the strap. He paused. Then....... JUMP! His hands barely missed the strap, adding to his already growing irritation. He growled with frustration, as he dipped down for another attempt.

This time he reached the strap and for a second swings in the air before the door slides down enough for his feet to touch the ground. Then his outstretched body slowly brought the door down to close the truck. The door clicked, as it reached the lock. Then he grabbed the rectangular metal handle and turned it to the left to finish locking the door. He walked back down the steps and climbed into the truck. Just before he pulled off, he sat quietly. He took one more deep breath, then put the truck in gear. The truck groaned to move forward. Black smoke scurried out of the back of the truck, as the cumbersome vehicle pulled away from the building. The mints rattled quietly in the darkness of the box. Occasionally, the box would bump up and down, then settle back into the low vibrations and rumbling of the truck. The pig sat quiet and still wondering what was going to happen next. Could it be any worst then what he has already encountered? Just when it started to seem like an eternity in the box, the pig could hear the sounds of the truck changing. The brakes began to squeak as the truck dropped its speed. The driver turned into the parking lot of a lone grocery store with a pasture surrounding it. The parking lot had six parking spaces in the front. The asphalt was freshly paved and the lines marking the spaces where bright white as they reflected the remaining morning sun. The modest store had a porch in the front with two rocking chairs slowly tilting from the light breeze blowing, as the morning turned to afternoon.

Maurice Bennett ©2007

The breeze also triggered a little wind chime that was hanging from the corner of the roof. The light sounds added a subtle peacefulness to this quaint little store. The driver hopped out of the cab and walked to the back to unload the boxes. The back door slammed open, startling the pig. Suddenly, the box dropped quickly then stopped. The mints flew everywhere in the box, reacting to the sudden movement. Then the box slowly dropped, as the driver put it onto a hand truck sitting next to the bumper. He climbed up and put two more boxes on top of the first box. Then he jumped down and started pulling the boxes into the store. There was a ramp in front of the store with two metal rails on each side. The paint was bright and fresh, making the rails shine like new. The driver went up the ramp and into the store.

A bell dinged as the door is opened. A man's voice said, "Put them in the back Frank!" The store was small yet spacious. The isles were narrow but not cramped. There were only three isles in the entire store and a few displays. The walls had pictures of rolling hills and scenery all over. A stuffed dear head hung from the wall over a few hunting supplies and the whole place smelled like leather and cookies. The driver yelled back to the man, "Is your wife baking?!"

BEER

FLOUR FLOUR

FLOUR FLOUR

Maurice Bennett © 2007

The voice replied, "Yeah! She just made a whole batch of them snicker doodles. There's some over there on the counter by the register. Help yourself when you walk by!" A candy display was right by the door as the driver came in. Before he started walking, he reached behind the door, took a few mints from the display, and nonchalantly dropped them into his pocket. He walked towards the back of the store. Just before he passed the counter he stopped and looked at the cookies. He looked at his hands, which had smudges and patches of dust on them. He mumbled to himself, "I'll grab them on the way out."

He went to the back and un-stacked the boxes one by one. The back room was very small. A bunch of various sized boxes were stacked and placed everywhere. It was dark and the translucent windows let very little light in. He just slid the three boxes in front of the rest of the boxes, grabbed his hand truck, and started back to the front. The hand truck rattled, as it went across the tile floor. The driver stopped at the cookies again. He took his hand and brushed it briskly across his pants. Then he looked at it again, examining it in the fluorescent light from the ceiling. He grabbed a cookie. He paused to look back in consideration of another cookie but he said, "I don't need it." He left the store with a slight smile on his face. The door dinged as he exits.

Meanwhile the pig is once again settling into the silent darkness of the box. Suddenly he heard footsteps coming closer. A voice said, "This must be that candy I ordered from that new factory down the road. I sure hope these mints are worth it. My other mints are from last Christmas and I still haven't sold out." Then.......SHKRRRRRRRT! Kkt.........Kkt. The box opened. The light flooded in forcing the pig to close his eyes, to adjust to the bright light. Everything is blurry, as the pig's eyes strained to focus. It's like he has never seen light before. A shadow appeared in the light. The pig could tell it was a man, as everything came into focus and little details could be seen. Through thick, magnifying glasses a pair of old weathered eyes examined the pig. He was wearing a plaid, short sleeved shirt tucked into a pair of gray slacks. His shoes were brown and worn from a long time of use. His skinny, frail hands were shaking as they held the little candy coated pig in the light.

His hair was short and white all over yet it covered his whole head. His sunken in mouth quivered to form words. "What's this?" The man asked himself. "This isn't what I ordered. I guess it's some kinda promotional thing. They are always trying something new. Why don't they just stick to the ol' school mint. A little mint in a clear plastic wrapper. What do they have now? Some kinda......uh....uh....Pig-mint! Shucks..... What will they think of next? I guess I'll put it out anyway." He placed the pig back in the box and picked the whole box up. Normally the pig would have tried to flee, but he couldn't really move. And the candy still kept his lips together, like they were glued. All he could do is watch as the box tilted back and forth from the old man carrying the mints to the front. He put the box down in front of the candy display. "I guess I'll put the new Pig-mint up front so the customers can go ahead and buy him on off. Some kid will probably want him. I'll just mark him up ten cents, because he's new." He grabbed the pig and stuck a bright orange sticker marked sixty cents on his head. He placed him on the display shelf. He slowly dumped the rest of the mints in the bin below the shelf, with a small scoop. He also placed some candy in three clear jars with lids. The jars had the same orange sticker, but they read a dollar fifty. Once he finished, he put the scoop back into the bin, grabbed the box and walked to the back. As he was walking, he started to unfold the box and flatten it out. The pig could hear his coughs echo from the back of the store.

Soon, the pig began to gaze out of the front window. The rolling pasture across the road reminded him of the old times at the farm. The pasture is green and peaceful. Little white butterflies frolic in their freedom, as they play atop the long grass. Back home there was a pond just on the other side of the pasture. The greatest mud wallows in the world. He remembered how cool the mud felt on a hot summer day, while he was out on walks with the kids. The times were so simple then. Now I'm stuck in an invisible blanket with candy all over me, the pig thought. As he continued gazing out of the window, a mini van slows down in front of the store. A little light blinking on the front of the van snapped the pig out of his daze. The vehicle turned into the lot and parked in the space next to the ramp. Both doors opened at the same time to release the van's passengers. Two little feet, wearing sandals, dropped out from behind one of the doors. The door revealed a little girl wearing a white dress with flowers around the edge of the bottom. Her brown curls spring up and down as she looked back to close the door. She put two hands on the door and closed it firmly. The other door revealed a woman wearing jeans and a yellow top with straps over the shoulder. She's carrying a brown purse which she tucked under her arm as she approached the store. "C'mon sweetie." The woman said. Her boots were noisy on the new parking lot. The little girl galloped behind the woman up the ramp to the store.

DING! The door announced the two customers. "OH OH! MOM! Can I have some candy?!" The little girl asked abruptly. "No sweetheart. Mom has plenty of snacks at home that you still have to eat. Not to mention this cake I'm gonna bake for my little princess." The mother said with a smile. "C'mon now this is just a quick stop for some cake mix." The mother walked to the second isle and began to pick out the mix. The little girl kept standing next to the candy display. She started looking through the bin of mints like she was trying to select the perfect mint. Every few moments she would pick up a mint then put it back down. Shortly, her face saddened subtly to acknowledge her disappointment. Then her gaze slowly moved up to the shelf and onto the jars with mints in them. The little pig froze. Hoping the little girl would not see him. If she found out he was a real pig, he would be in big trouble or worst. She slowly went from one jar to the next then…."MOM! Come here! Come quick!" The mother walked over to the display to attend to the little girl. "What are we looking at here?" The little girl pointed at the pig. The pig stayed frozen. "Look. They have a Pig-mint!" The mother said, "Oh. I didn't know they made those. It must be something else new they've come out with." The little girl said, "Can we get him? Look mom he's only sixty cents!" The mother said, "Hmmmm. Sixty cents huh? Welll…" The girl interrupted, "Please, please, please, please!"

51

She began to dance back and fourth as her mother pondered the purchase. "Welllll……..I guess he is pretty cute. Being that he's a pig and mint and all. Okay. You talked me into it." "YAY!" The little girl exclaimed.

The mother grabbed the little pig off the shelf and handed him to the little girl. Her fingers wiggled with excitement, as she grabbed the pig. The mother walked back to the isle with the girl in toe. "Devils food?......yellow cake mix.….lemon.….angel food. Okay. Angel food for an angel." The mother said looking at her daughter smiling. "At least that's what my mom used to tell me." She said sarcastically. The mother grabbed the box of cake mix and went to the counter. The old man heard the mother and child come in and was waiting behind the counter. He had one of the cookies on a napkin in front of him. His jaws were still moving from already having eaten a cookie. Crumbs were on the sides of his mouth. "How you doing?" he said to the mother. "Fine, fine. We just came in for some cake mix." The mother confessed. "CAKE MIX!? On a Monday?....I guess everyone is in a baking mood today. My wife baked these cookies this morning. I figured I would bring them in today and share with the customers. You're welcome to help yerself." He said. "Thank you. But I'll pass. I gotta save room for this cake I'm gonna bake for this lovely lady here."

53

She replied. "She is a lovely little lady isn't she? Ma'am would you like an old fashioned snicker doodle?" He asked the little girl. "No thanks. I'm saving room for this." The little girl held the awkward candy pig up. "Whatchu got there?" The old man said as he leaned in close to see. "Oh yeah! That's that Pig-mint candy isn't it? Yeah I knew someone would probably want him. The factory must be trying something new I guess. I heard that they taste pretty good." "Really?!" The little girl replied. "Oh yes! Now let me see….. you got some angel food cake mix, for a couple of angels." The old man said, as he gives the mother a wink. "And a brand new candy Pig-mint." He said, while typing the prices into the register. "Your total is a dollar eighty two."

The mother smiled, handed the old man two dollars and grabbed the bag off the counter. She handed the little pig to the girl. As she turned towards the door she said, " Keep the change!" He replied, "Allllllrighty. You have a good day and drive safely." The door dinged as it announced the departure of the customers.

The door locks clicked, as the mother approached the van with her keys jingling. The little girl opened the door with one hand and the Pig-mint in the other. She put the pig in the seat first. Then she climbed in and gently moved him into her lap. She grabbed the seat belt and pulled it across her and the pig. Then she waited for her mother to finish getting in.

The pig continued to remain still, because the humans haven't found out he's a real pig. He has to wait until they leave. But......what if they never leave? The pig thought. The mother got in, fastened her seat belt, and cranked the vehicle. She put her purse in the back seat and put her sunglasses on. She asked the little girl, "You ready for take off?" The little girl said, "Roger!" The mother put the van in gear. She looked both ways then proceeded to back out into the road. As the van pulled off, the pig began to settle into the little girls lap, as it reminded him of when he was very young and the kids use to let him ride in the wagon. They put him in their lap and rode down the hill in a shiny red wagon. He remembered how warm and safe he felt. Will he ever be back there again? He began to gaze out of the window, as the docile countryside passed by. What else could possibly happen to me? The pig wondered.

THE END

Thanks

To all who have supported me and encouraged
me to follow my dreams. This accomplishment
shows the power of encouragement. I send
many thanks to my father: Dwain, mother: Tanya,
brother: Taire. Dorene. Friends: Rob, James, Randall,
Ron, Chris and Tony for their support.
Thank you all.

www.ingramcontent.com/pod-product-compliance
Lightning Source LLC
Chambersburg PA
CBHW040830050726
47507CB00021B/172